Chapter 1
Splish! Splash!

"Arrr! Row! Row! Row!" Rotten Tooth shouted as the little dinghy made its way over the waves. Each time he shouted, the rest of us pirates on board the little boat had to pull back on the oars as hard as we could.

"Blimey, being a pirate kid sure is hard work sometimes," I said.

"Aye, Pete, and splashy work," Gary added.

Gary was my best mate at Pirate School. We both had light-colored hair. And we both wore pirate hats. But unlike me, Gary was a little clumsy. So every time he pulled on the oar, he got splashed in the face. And since we were sharing an oar with our friend Inna, it meant she got a little splashed, too.

"Arrr! Maybe if you weren't such a blunder head, it wouldn't be so splashy!" Inna shouted. She was the only pirate kid I knew who didn't like to get splashed. She was also the only pirate kid I ever met who brushed her hair and wore pretty dresses. She said splashing ruined both.

Some of the splashing even reached our friends Aaron and Vicky. They were sharing an oar behind us.

"I don't mind the splashing," Vicky said.

I didn't mind it, either. It was hot in the morning sun and the splashing felt good.

We were part of our ship's landing party. That meant we had to row the little boat all the way to the beach. But it also meant that once we made it to the beach, we got to help look for treasure.

"ROW! ROW! ROW!" Rotten Tooth shouted again. He was standing right behind us and didn't have to row at all. That's because he was in charge of the dinghy and the landing party. The pirate in charge never has to row. It's in the pirate code. In my nine and three-quarters years, I've learned all about the pirate code.

"ROW! ROW! Row with all your might, mateys!" Rotten Tooth yelled. I wished I didn't have to hold both hands on the oar. Rotten Tooth's breath was so stinky, I wanted to cover my nose.

"One day, I'm going to be the pirate in charge. Then I won't have to row," I said to my friends.

"Aye," Vicky said. "Never mind the splashing—rowing is the part I don't like."

"Aye," Gary said as the oar splashed us again.

Inna wiped the water away from her face. "I don't like either part!" she exclaimed.

"Quit bellyaching," Aaron said.

Aaron was Vicky's twin brother. They looked exactly alike. They even dressed alike. They both had dark hair and dark eyes. They wore matching red-and-white-

5

striped clothes. The only thing that was different was that Aaron was a boy. And he was a show-off, too.

"Rowing is easy breezy," he said.

Vicky gave him a long look. Aaron was leaning back with both hands behind his head.

"Arrr!" she growled. "That's because you're not even rowing!"

"Aye! That's what makes it so easy," he said.

Vicky was just about to say something else when Rotten Tooth leaned over and yelled into Aaron's ear. "ARRR! Get to rowing, ye scurvy pup, or ye'll be shark bait!" he shouted.

Aaron gulped!

"Aye aye!" he said. He grabbed the oar and started rowing like the rest of us.

"Arrr, that's what I thought," Rotten Tooth snarled.

Rotten Tooth was the meanest pirate on the seas. He was also the ugliest! He had a pointy green beard and green teeth, too.

Plus, he was our teacher and the first mate of our ship, the *Sea Rat*. That meant he was the double boss of us, so it wasn't a good idea to make him mad.

"Blimey, I hate rowing," Aaron mumbled once Rotten Tooth wasn't paying attention anymore.

Vicky stuck her tongue out at him. "Arrr! I told you so," she said.

I lifted up my pirate hat and took a look ahead.

"Avast! It won't be much longer," I told my friends. The beach was getting closer each time we rowed. "Besides, it'll all be worth it when we reach land. Once we get ashore, we'll be looking for buried treasure!"

"Aye!" my friends agreed.

Looking for buried treasure was one of the most fun parts about being a pirate. This was the first time since we came to Pirate School that Captain Stinky Beard picked us to be part of the landing party. He said we'd proven that we were brave pirates.

Rotten Tooth wasn't so sure. If it were up to him, he wouldn't teach us anything except how to swab the deck. Lucky for us, the cap'n was the boss of him.

"I hope we find the treasure first," Vicky said.

"Aye!" I agreed.

"That'll show old Rotten Head," Aaron said.

"Aye aye!" Gary said as he splashed Inna again by accident. The rest of us couldn't keep from giggling when we saw how soggy she was.

Inna wasn't giggling.

She gave Gary a grumpy look. "Arrr, I just hope we get there before you sink the whole boat," she grumbled.

Chapter 2
Digging Is the Pits!

Vicky leaned against her shovel and crossed her arms. "Great sails! You'll never find the treasure that way," she yelled at Aaron.

The beach around us was covered with tiny holes that Aaron had dug. They were more like dents than holes. The rest of us were digging holes as deep as we were tall!

"You have to dig bigger holes!" Vicky told him.

Aaron folded his arms and lifted his chin in the air. That was the face he always made when he was being a know-it-all. He made that face a lot.

"Arrr! I was just starting the holes for the rest of you guys," Aaron said.

"Aye, because that's the easiest part!" Vicky shouted.

"Is not!" Aaron said.

"IS TOO!" Vicky shouted.

Then she marched over to Aaron and gave him a tiny shove.

I didn't like it when my friends were fighting. So I ran over and stood between them. "Shiver me timbers! That's no way to act on our first real pirate mission," I shouted.

Aaron and Vicky forgot they were angry with each other and turned on me.

"Real pirate mission? That's hogwash!" Aaron said. "Rotten Tooth only agreed to let us come along so we could row and carry shovels."

"Aye!" Vicky shouted. "That's why he stuck us here while the rest of the crew is way down there on the other end of the beach. That's where Rotten Tooth thinks the treasure is!"

"Aye aye!" Inna said. "The only thing I've found is sand!"

"Me too," Gary said. "I even found sand in my skivvies." Then he jumped around and tried to shake the sand out of his pants.

"Aye. Maybe Rotten Tooth sent us here so we wouldn't find the treasure, but Captain Stinky Beard said the treasure map wasn't very clear," I reminded them. "That means the treasure could be anywhere on this beach! It's our pirate duty to help find it!"

My friends scratched their heads. That meant they were thinking really hard about what I'd said. They also scratched their bellies, their arms, and their legs. But that had nothing to do with thinking. It just meant that the sand was very itchy.

"Arrr, maybe Pete's right," Vicky said when she was done scratching.

"Aye," Inna agreed. "Pirate duty is serious business. Maybe we should stop bellyaching and start digging again."

"Arrr! And digging sure beats rowing," Aaron said.

"Aye," Gary added. "At least we can take breaks and build sand castles."

"That's the spirit, mateys," I said. "We'll find the treasure first and prove we're the best pirates on the seas, even if we are only kids!"

Then we all put our hands together in a circle and gave our pirate cheer. "Swashbuckling, sailing, finding treasure, too. Becoming pirates is what we want to do!"

We picked up our shovels and started digging again.

Everyone except Gary. He was too busy jumping around trying to get the sand out of his skivvies. He jumped around so much that his glasses fell off. When he bent down to pick them up, he tripped over his shovel.

THUMP!

He tripped right into Inna.

Then . . . CRASH!

They both tumbled into a big hole that Vicky had dug.

I ran over to the hole and peeked in.

"Blimey! Are you guys okay?" I asked.

I thought for sure Inna was going to pull Gary's hat down over his ears and bop him on the head. That's what she always did when Gary made her mad. Only when I poked my head down, Inna didn't look mad at all. She was actually smiling!

Aaron and Vicky rushed over to me. They peeked in, too. "She must have bumped her head a little too hard!" Aaron suggested when he saw Inna smiling.

"Aye," I agreed.

"I didn't bump anything," Inna hollered. Then we watched as she brushed away the sand under her feet. "I'm smiling because I think we found something!"

Gary helped her brush away the sand. They were both standing on something. And when all the sand was brushed away, we saw what it was.

One giant treasure chest, just like Captain Stinky Beard had said!

"HOORAY!" We all let out a great big cheer.

Aaron, Vicky, and I danced around outside the hole. Inna and Gary danced around inside the hole. Then instead of bopping Gary on the head, Inna gave him a hug.

Sometimes being clumsy was the same as being lucky!

Chapter 3
Something Fishy!

"Arrr! The last one there is seaweed slime!" Vicky called out as she ran across the beach.

"Aye! You better get ready to be slimed then," I hollered.

I was right behind her, running as fast as I could. We were racing to tell Rotten Tooth the good news.

Aaron stayed behind to guard the treasure. Inna and Gary stayed behind, too. They weren't really guarding. They were just too small to climb out of the hole.

"Avast! There he is," I said as soon as I saw Rotten Tooth.

Vicky and I ran faster.

We were so busy racing, we forgot to

look where we were going. So we didn't see
Rotten Tooth step in front of us until it
was too late.

DOUBLE CRASH!

"Arrr! What's gotten into ye pollywogs?"
Rotten Tooth roared.

We gulped!

Rotten Tooth looked even madder
than the time Aaron was pretending to
swashbuckle and buckled him right in the
tummy!

"We're sorry," I said. "We were racing."

"Racing?" Rotten Tooth bellowed.

"Aye," Vicky admitted. "Did you see who won?"

"ARRR! Ye both lost!" he growled. "When we get back to the *Sea Rat*, ye'll be racing to see who can wash the most dishes!"

"But we were racing to tell you something important," I said.

"Aye?" Rotten Tooth asked.

"AYE!" Vicky said. "We found the treasure!"

The rest of the landing party stopped digging and turned to look at us. They dropped their shovels and cheered. "Hooray for our little shipmates!"

I couldn't tell if they were happy because we found the treasure or because they didn't have to dig anymore. Probably both.

Rotten Tooth was the only one who didn't look happy. He thought us pirate kids were only good for being deckhands.

He didn't like it one bit when we did shipshape pirate work.

"Arrr, ye better show me," he grumbled. "And ye better not be fibbing, or else!"

"Nope. No fibbing," I said. Then I grabbed one of his hands and Vicky grabbed the other. Together, we brought him back to where our friends were waiting.

Only when we got there, we didn't see any of our friends. We only saw a bunch of holes.

"Arrr! I don't have time for games," Rotten Tooth barked.

"But it's not a game," I said. "They were just here."

Vicky crossed her arms and frowned. "I bet this is all Aaron's fault," she mumbled. She always thought everything that went wrong was Aaron's fault.

Just then, we heard a scream coming from one of the holes.

"INNA!" I shouted.

We followed the screams. They were coming from the hole where we had found the treasure.

19

"Shiver me timbers!" Vicky yelled when she peeked into the hole.

"Aye!" I said. My timbers were shivering, too! That's because not only were our friends in the hole, so was a giant sand crab! It was almost as big as Gary!

Inna was covering her eyes. She didn't like crabs at all. She said they were the same as spiders, only worse. And she thought spiders were the second-scariest thing in the world besides snakes.

Gary didn't have to cover his eyes. He still didn't have his glasses on, so he didn't know what was happening.

"Arrr! This is our treasure, you scallywag!" Aaron yelled as he tried to hold the crab back with a shovel. But the giant crab grabbed the shovel with its claw and snapped it in half!

"Stand back," Rotten Tooth said. Then he reached down

20

and picked up that pinchy crab by the back legs! He swung it around and around over his head, then tossed it into the sea.

My mouth dropped wide open!

"Arrr! He might be mean, but Rotten Tooth sure is one brave pirate," I whispered to Vicky.

"Aye." She nodded.

"Arrr! Don't stand there like barnacles," Rotten Tooth said to us. "Help your little mates out while I get the treasure."

"Aye aye!" we said, and gave Rotten Tooth a pirate salute.

Aaron gave Inna and Gary a boost while Vicky and I pulled them up. Rotten Tooth lifted the treasure chest out of the hole. Then he lifted Aaron out, too. Before long, everyone had two feet on the ground . . . even the giant sand crab!

"It's back!" Inna shouted, pointing to the crab crawling toward us.

"Aye, and it brought friends," I said, pointing at an army of crabs marching behind it.

Rotten Tooth scooped up the treasure chest and pointed to the rest of the crew. "Let's go, buckoes!" he ordered.

We all hurried as fast as we could. It was like the race Vicky and I had run, except that this time, the last one there would be crab bait for real!

"All hands back to the *Sea Rat*!" Rotten Tooth hollered. The crew loaded the boats as quickly as they could. Then we leaped on and started to row away. By the time we were out to sea, the beach was covered with sand crabs.

"That was a close one," I whispered.

"Aye," Inna said. "It almost pinched us in two!"

"Lucky for you mates, I was there," Aaron said. For once, being a show-off had actually come in handy.

"But what were those crabs there for in the first place?" Vicky asked.

"I heard a pirate tale on my old ship about crabs that guarded treasure," Gary told us. He had heard tons of pirate tales.

The ship he was on before the *Sea Rat* had an entire library of tales, and Gary had heard all about them.

"Aye?" we asked.

"Aye!" Gary said. "It said crabs guard only cursed treasure!"

We all made spooky *ooohhh* and *aaahhh* noises. That's because cursed treasure was super-spooky business.

Rotten Tooth heard us whispering. He had the best hearing of any pirate ever born. He could hear a mouse snoring even if it was on a ship anchored two days away!

"Stow that talk," he roared at us. "There's no such thing as cursed treasure. Those are just tales to scare wee pups like ye lot."

"Aye?" I asked.

"AYE!" he yelled. "And ye better not go blabbing to the cap'n about curses and crabs! 'Tis bad luck, ye savvy?"

"Aye," we mumbled. No sailor wanted to bring bad luck to their ship.

"Now if ye don't mind," Rotten Tooth said, "ROW! ROW! ROW!"

Chapter 4
Finders Keepers

"Shipshape work, matey!" Captain Stinky Beard said as Rotten Tooth unloaded the treasure chest onto the deck of the *Sea Rat*.

"'Twas no work at all, Cap'n!" Rotten Tooth bragged.

"Aye, because he didn't do any work to find it," Vicky whispered.

I covered my mouth to keep from giggling. It wasn't polite to giggle while the captain was on deck. That was in the pirate code.

"With that spotty map, I thought it would take twice as long to find this here treasure," Captain Stinky Beard said. "I'm very impressed."

That made my friends and me smile real proud.

But then our smiles disappeared because Rotten Tooth took all the credit. "Aye, it was right where I thought it would be," he told the captain.

I crossed my arms and made a huff.

"Arrr! That stinks worse than the fish gut tank," I whispered to my friends. Then I held my nose and pretended to smell the worst smell I ever smelled.

"Aye," my friends agreed.

"We should tell the captain the truth," Gary whispered.

"Aye, but Rotten Tooth would make us walk the plank if we did," Inna said.

"Aye! Plus, if we tattle on him, he'll make us do chores for the rest of our lives," I added. "And chores can sometimes be worse than walking the plank!"

The only thing we could do was moan and groan. But once Captain Stinky Beard opened the treasure chest, we didn't feel like moaning or groaning anymore. The treasure was so shiny and sparkly that we forgot all about how rotten old Rotten Tooth was.

"Sink me!" I said. "That's the richest treasure I've ever seen."

"Aye aye!" Vicky said.

Then Captain Stinky Beard told every member of the landing party to form a line. "It be a pirate tradition that every pirate who finds a treasure gets to keep one piece of it," he said.

"Arrr!" I whispered to my friends. "That's how I got my lucky pirate hat."

"Aye, and that's how I got my shiny necklace," Inna told us proudly.

"That's how Aaron and I got our matching belt buckles, too," Vicky said. Then she and Aaron pushed their bellies out to show us their silver star belt buckles.

"Once I got a golden goblet that way," Gary told us. "Then I buried it and made a map."

"Aye? Where is it?" I asked.

Gary scratched his head and shrugged. "I don't know," he said. "I buried the map with the goblet by accident."

Aaron burst out laughing. "You must be daft to lose something that important."

"You lose stuff, too, Captain Big Mouth," Vicky said. That's the name she called Aaron when he acted like he was better than everyone else.

"Arrr! I never lost anything," Aaron told her.

"Aye? What about that time on our last ship when we went swimming and you lost your skivvies?" Vicky asked him. "You had to wear a leaf for two hours until you found them again!"

Aaron turned bright red. "Oh, yeah, I forgot about that time," he said.

"Well, nobody's going to lose anything this time," I said. "And even if one of us does, the rest of us will be there to help find it. That's what best mates do!"

"Aye aye!" everyone agreed.

Then we began to think about which

piece of treasure we would choose once it was our turn to pick. The chest was full of medallions, rings, necklaces, jewels, coins, and everything else that we pirates loved. Since we were the youngest, we were last in line. That gave us plenty of time to decide.

By the time we got to the front of the line, Captain Stinky Beard had gone back to his quarters and the others had all gone back to their posts. Rotten Tooth was the only one left standing near the treasure.

"Pirate Pete reporting for treasure pickup!" I said with a smile. Then I pointed to a set of silver boot buckles. "We'd each like one of those, please," I said. There were five sets and we'd all decided to get matching treasure.

Rotten Tooth snatched all five sets and then slammed the treasure chest closed. Then he shoved the boot buckles into his pocket. "I'll be holding onto these for safekeeping," he snarled.

"ARRR! That's no fair!" Vicky shouted.

"Aye! We earned those," I said.

"Aye, and ye will most likely lose them, too," Rotten Tooth growled.

"Hogwash! I've never lost anything!" Aaron said.

"Aye?" Rotten Tooth asked. "Not even your skivvies while you were swimming one time?"

Aaron crossed his arms and frowned. "Soggy sails! He hears everything!" he grumbled.

"Aye, that's right," Rotten Tooth said.

"It's still not fair," I said. "We found the treasure in the first place!"

"And ye will get your treasure," Rotten Tooth growled. "Once ye be real pirates instead of wee sprogs, that's when I'll give ye your treasure."

"We are real pirates!" Inna shouted. "You just don't want us to have them because you're a dirty rascal!"

We all gulped!

Inna was a real brave pirate sometimes. Sure, she was afraid of lots of things, but she wasn't afraid of Rotten Tooth. I never

30

heard anyone call Rotten Tooth names to his face before.

She crossed her arms and huffed. "Maybe we should report you to the cap'n," she suggested.

Rotten Tooth twisted his face into a scary grin. "I'll make ye mangy pups a deal," he said. "Ye keep your traps shut and tomorrow I'll teach ye how to swashbuckle."

"SWASHBUCKLE?" we all shouted in surprise.

Swashbuckling was best pirate skill there was. Rotten Tooth had never taught us anything exciting before. If he was really going to teach us how to swashbuckle, it was worth a few boot buckles.

"Deal?" he asked.

"Deal!" we agreed.

Then we raced belowdecks to our room. The next day of Pirate School was going to be the best day ever. We could hardly wait for it to be morning again.

Chapter 5
Abandoned Ship?

"Blimey! What's that stink?" I asked the next morning as we headed to the mess hall for breakfast.

Inna pinched her nose and stuck out her tongue. "It smells like rotten fish."

"I hope that's not breakfast," Gary said.

"Me too," Vicky said.

"Me three," Aaron said.

We went into the kitchen and saw a pot on the stove. I lifted the lid and took a peek inside. It was the seaweed gruel the crew had eaten for dinner the night before. We were too tired from all the rowing and digging to eat. We had fallen asleep before dinner. By the looks of it, it was lucky we did.

"YUCK!" I said. My face turned as green

as the mush inside the pot.

Inna pointed to the stack of dirty dishes piled up to the ceiling. "DOUBLE YUCK!" she said. Then she covered her mouth to keep from being sick. No one had cleaned up and the leftovers had turned gruesome!

"Arrr! I think I lost my appetite," Gary said.

"Aye, me too," Vicky said.

"I wonder why no one cooked this morning. Or cleaned up last night?" Vicky asked.

"Arrr! That's pretty fishy," I said.

"Who cares? Today we get to learn how to swashbuckle!" Aaron shouted excitedly. Then he picked up a mop and started to swing it around like a sword. I had to duck to keep from being buckled on the head.

I rolled my eyes. "Aye, and you have a lot to learn!" I said.

Vicky giggled. "Aye, you can say that again!"

Aaron frowned. "I still know more than you," he argued.

"Do not!" Vicky told him.

"Do too!" Aaron told her right back.

I held up my hands to make them stop. "Why don't we go above deck and find out who knows what?"

"Aye! Besides, it's too stinky to stay in here," Inna added.

"Aye!" Vicky said. "Let's race to the main deck!" Then she took off to get a head start.

34

"Gangway!" Aaron shouted, and took off after her.

Inna, Gary, and I followed them, but we didn't race. We wanted to save our energy for our swashbuckling lesson.

When we climbed the galley stairs, Aaron and Vicky were waiting for us on the main deck. They were bickering about who had won the race. They were so busy arguing that they didn't notice that we were the only pirates in sight.

No pirates were manning the sails.

No pirates were manning the rigging.

No pirates were swabbing the deck.

There were no pirates anywhere!

"Great sails!" I shouted. "Where's the crew?"

Aaron and Vicky stopped fighting and looked around.

Inna scratched her head.

Gary spun around in circles.

Not a single one of us spied another member of the crew. The deck of the *Sea Rat* was absolutely, positively abandoned!

Chapter 6
Seasick Sailors

"Arrr! This must be some kind of trick," Vicky said.

"Aye! I bet Rotten Tooth is hiding so he doesn't have to teach us how to swashbuckle," Aaron said with a growl.

I wasn't so sure.

"What about the rest of the crew?" I asked.

Just then a voice boomed from behind us. "Arrr! Most of the crew be sick as dogs!"

We spun around and saw Rotten Tooth standing behind us. His face was as green as his beard! It made him look even scarier than usual.

"Sick?" Gary asked. "Blimey! How did everyone get sick?"

"Maybe it was the seaweed slop," Inna said. Then she stuck out her tongue because just thinking about it was making her sickish.

"Aye," Rotten Tooth groaned. Then he ran over to the railing and got sick himself. When he was done, he looked worse than ever. "Whatever it was, it sure be a powerful sickness," he told us.

Aaron stomped his foot. "Arrr! Does this mean we're not going to learn how to swashbuckle?" he asked.

"This means you're not going to learn anything today, mateys," Rotten Tooth said. "School's canceled!" Then he leaned over the railing again.

We all turned away.

"I'm glad we're not icky sicky," Vicky said.

"Aye!" Gary agreed. "Last time I was icky sicky, I was icky sicky all over my shirt."

Rotten Tooth stumbled over to us. He was so sick, he couldn't stand up straight! "Arrr!

37

Ye pollywogs will need to man the deck,"
he said.

"All by ourselves?" Vicky asked.

We all gulped!

Manning the ship was an extra-big job.

"No, no! There be a few others to help,"
Rotten Tooth said. He pointed toward the
galley stairs, where a few other pirates
were making their way on deck.

"Avast! That's the night crew!" I said.
The night crew never eats dinner with the
rest of the crew. So they didn't look sick,
but they did look tired. That's because they
usually sleep all day.

"Don't they need to rest?" Inna asked.

"Arrr! Not as much as I do," Rotten
Tooth roared before racing back to the
railing. We covered our eyes. It made us
sickish just watching him.

"That's what he gets for double-crossing
us," Vicky whispered.

"Aye," I whispered back.

"I'm heading back to my quarters,"
Rotten Tooth told us. Then he ordered us

to get to work. "Ye pups are always saying you're real pirates, so prove it!" After that, he disappeared down the galley stairs.

I looked at my friends.

Then I looked at all the sails and ropes and everything else that needed to be manned. Most of the night crew that came above deck were already snoring at their posts!

"Mateys, this is going to be hard work," I said.

"Aye!" Vicky agreed. "Even harder than rowing!"

"Or digging," Aaron added.

"Or eating that gruesome gruel," Inna said.

"It's going to be impossible!" Gary exclaimed.

"But the ship needs us," I said. "It's our duty to try our best!"

"Aye aye!" everyone agreed.

We didn't waste another second. We each ran to a different post and tried our best to keep the *Sea Rat* on course.

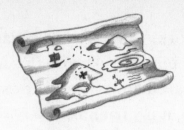

Chapter 7
Sailing in Circles!

"I said hoist the sail, not *moist* the sail!" Vicky shouted at Aaron. She was furious! Instead of raising the sail to make the ship go faster, Aaron had soaked it with a bucket of water.

"Yo-ho-ho! What's the big deal?" Aaron asked.

Vicky made her hands into fists. "Wet sails make the ship go slower—that's what the big deal is!" she roared. "Everyone knows that!"

"Arrr! Who says we need to go faster?" Aaron shouted back.

"Aye! We don't even know where we're heading," Gary said.

My friends stopped doing their jobs and

stared at him. I kept
manning the steering
wheel and tried to
keep the ship straight.
   "What do you
mean?" Inna asked
Gary. "You're the one
with the map! You're supposed to plot our
course!"

   "Aye," Gary admitted. "But when I went
into Captain Stinky Beard's quarters, I
wasn't sure which map to take. And since
he's sick, too, I couldn't ask him."

   "Arrr! There are a lot of maps in there,"
I said, trying to stick up for Gary.

   "Aye, but it's always the one on top!"
Inna shouted.

   I reached under my pirate hat and
scratched my head. "That makes sense," I
said. Inna sure was one clever pirate kid.
"Maybe we should have asked you to get
the map," I said.

   "AYE! Then my dress wouldn't have
gotten all ruined from these slimy ropes,"

Inna said. She'd been working with Vicky to man the ropes. There were ropes tangled all around her. They'd made her dress all muddy and yucky.

"I'm sorry," Gary said.

Inna reached over and pulled his hat down over his ears and bopped him on the head. "There! Now you're sorry."

I waved my hand up in the air to get everyone's attention. "Mateys, now's not the time for fighting," I said.

Gary wiggled his pirate hat over his ears again. "Aye. Fighting hurts my head."

"It was your head that got us in this mess in the first place," Aaron said.

"Aye! We don't even know if we're using the right map," Vicky said.

"Arrr! You didn't let me finish," Gary said. "I found the right map eventually."

"Then why did you say we didn't know where we were heading?" Aaron asked.

"Because," Gary explained, "when I came back on deck, the wind blew the map out of my hands. Now I don't know which way is up and which way is down."

Inna reached over to grab his hat again, but Gary stepped away just in time.

I took the map from Gary and looked at it. Then I turned it upside down and looked at again. I wasn't the best at reading maps. It looked the same both ways.

"Blimey! Give me that," Inna said. She took the map out of my hands. She was the best map reader out of all of us. "It goes this way," she said. "Now, where is the *Sea Rat*?" she asked Gary.

Gary shrugged. "I think here," he said, pointing to a spot on the map that looked

 like smooth sailing.

I wiped my forehead. "That's good news," I said.

"Aye," Vicky agreed.

"Aye," Gary said. "But we might also be

here!" Then he pointed to a spot on the map that wasn't smooth sailing.

"Avast!" Inna shouted. "If we're there, we're sailing right into Serpent's Whirlpool!"

"Sink me!" I shouted. "No ship can survive Serpent's Whirlpool! The water spins around so fast, it can drown any ship!"

"Well, which is it?" Inna asked Gary.

"Beats me." Gary shrugged. "It depends on which way I was holding the map when I plotted the course."

"Um, I think I know," Aaron said as he glanced over the railing.

"Soggy sails! We don't have time for you to be a show-off," Vicky told him.

"I'm not," Aaron yelled. "I know because there it is! Serpent's Whirlpool dead ahead!"

We all looked out to sea.

Aaron was right. The water was starting to spin in circles. If we didn't change course, the *Sea Rat* was going to sink to the bottom of the sea!

Chapter 8
Crabby Clues!

"One, two, three . . . PULL!" I shouted.

Aaron, Vicky, Inna, and I pulled on the rope with all our might. We were trying to turn the mainsail and catch a gust of wind that would take us to safe waters. But no matter how hard we pulled, the sail wouldn't budge.

The ship was too much for us to man all by ourselves. We had tried to wake up the night crew. But once pirates start snoring, it's almost impossible to wake them up.

 "Serpent's Whirlpool is still dead ahead," Gary shouted from the steering wheel. He was on steering duty because we were afraid he'd get tangled in the ropes if he tried to help us.

"It's no use," Aaron said.

"Aye," Vicky agreed.

"But we have to do something," Inna said. "The *Sea Rat* is starting to sail in circles, which means we're caught in the whirlpool's current."

"Aye," I said. "We have no choice. We have to try and wake the crew. We need more pirates to help us."

"With all the racket ye be making, ye could wake the dead." A voice laughed behind us. It was Clegg. He was the oldest pirate on board. Plus, he was our friend.

"CLEGG!" I shouted. "We're glad to see you!"

"Aye," Vicky said. "And we're double glad to see you're not icky sicky."

"I'm fit as a whale, minus the eye, of course," he joked pointing to his patch that covered one of his eyes. Then he looked around the deck. "Are ye li'l shipmates the only ones manning the ship?" he asked.

"Aye!" I said.

"Well, except for the night crew, but they're all snoring," Inna said.

"The rest of the crew is seasick," Vicky explained.

"Except you," Aaron said.

"Aye," I said. "How come you're not sick?"

Clegg scratched his beard. "Same reason you're not sick, I suppose."

"You didn't eat the seaweed slop either?" I asked.

"No, I ate a heaping helping," he told us.

We all gulped!

"If it wasn't the slop, it must be something else," Vicky said.

"We need to remember

everything that happened yesterday, step by step," Inna said. "Then we can figure it out."

"First, we rowed all the way to shore," Vicky began.

"Aye," Inna said. "Then Gary splashed me." She still seemed a little bit angry about that.

"Aye, then he blundered into you and you tumbled into the hole," I said. Then I covered my mouth because remembering that made me giggle.

"Then I saved you from those stinky sand crabs that tried to attack our treasure," Aaron said.

"Hogwash! You mean Rotten Tooth saved *you* from those crabs!" Vicky reminded him.

"Same thing," Aaron said.

Vicky was about to argue with him, but Clegg interrupted.

"Hold on, buckoes, did ye say sand crabs attacked the treasure?" Clegg asked.

We nodded.

"Were they giant sand crabs?" he asked.

We nodded again. I even held my arms far

apart to show Clegg just how giant those crabs were.

"How did you know? Were you spying on the landing party?" Vicky asked.

Clegg shook his head. "I wish I were, matey," he said.

"What's that supposed to mean?" Inna asked.

"It means the crew is in serious danger," Clegg said. "Ye see, giant sand crabs only guard cursed treasure!"

We all double gulped!

"Gary was right! He knew those crabs were bad news!" I said.

"Ahoy! We're starting to spin faster!" Gary shouted as he tried to steer the *Sea Rat* out of the whirlpool.

"What are we going to do?" I asked.

"Let me see," Clegg said. "By chance, did every seasick pirate take a piece of the treasure?"

"Aye, except Rotten Tooth. He took six pieces," Vicky said.

We all made grumble noises because five

of those pieces were supposed to be ours.

"That's it, then. The treasure is making them sick," Clegg said.

We stopped grumbling right then. I guess Rotten Tooth stealing our boot buckles wasn't so bad after all. It kept us from being icky sicky.

"We need to get all those pieces back in the treasure chest!" I said.

"Aye aye!" my friends agreed.

"I'll stay here and man the wheel," Clegg told us. "Ye better hurry. And remember, if ye touch the treasure too long, ye will be as sick as the others."

We all made faces. None of us wanted to be icky sicky. Then we all put our hands in a circle and said our pirate cheer.

"Swashbuckling, sailing, finding treasure, too. Becoming pirates is what we want to do!" we shouted.

Then we split up to find every last piece of treasure before it was too late!

Chapter 9
Snoop and Sneak

"Shhhh!" Inna whispered with her finger pressed to her mouth. "We have to be extra quiet," she told us as we sneaked down the galley stairs to where the sleeping quarters were.

"Aye," I whispered back. "If any pirate catches us taking their treasure, we'll be shark bait."

"Sink me," Gary whispered. "We're only trying to help."

"Aye," I said. "But stealing is against the pirate code, even if it's for a good reason."

"What are we going to do when they wake up?" Gary asked. "Will we get in trouble?" If there was one thing Gary was afraid of, it was getting in trouble.

I shrugged. "We have to hope they'll believe us about the curse," I said.

"If you two don't stow it, we'll wake them up before we have the chance," Inna whisper-shouted at us.

Gary and I quickly covered our mouths.

"That's better," Inna said. Then she slowly pushed open the door to the main sleeping quarters. It creaked and squeaked, but the pirates inside didn't budge.

"Arrr, it looks like the curse has changed from seasick to sea sleep," Gary said. He was right, too. Every pirate inside was snoring away. But it wasn't the good kind of sleep. I could tell because every one of them was also green and sickish-looking.

Inna snooped over to one side of the room and Gary snooped to the other. I snooped right down the middle. We went from sickbed to sickbed, quietly snatching the pieces of treasure. The *Sea Rat* continued to sail around in circles faster and faster, and we had to try hard to keep our balance.

Inna finished her row first. She had bracelets dangling from both arms and necklaces all around her neck.

I finished my row second.

"Hurry up," Inna whispered to Gary. We had to be quick or we would be seasick, too.

Gary hurried as best he could. Only whenever Gary hurried, he got clumsy. I could see him getting clumsy as he tried to climb up the last bunk.

He wibbled and wobbled.

Inna and I covered our eyes and waited for the thump!

But that thump never came.

Gary never blundered!

"Done!" Gary said once he sneaked over to us.

"Good work," I said.

"Aye," Inna agreed. "Maybe you're not such a blunder head after all."

We were all happy. But our good cheer didn't last long. That's because with all the treasure we were carrying, we were starting to feel a little seasick.

"We have to hurry and get this back into the treasure chest before we get icky sicky all over the place," I said.

"Aye," Gary moaned.

"Aye, let's hope Vicky and Aaron were able to get the rest," Inna said.

When we got on deck, they weren't there yet.

"I hope they didn't get caught," I said. Vicky and Aaron had the most dangerous job. They had to scoop Captain Stinky

Beard's treasure away and Rotten Tooth's, too.

We put the treasure we were carrying back in the chest. It was just in time, too! I was starting to feel as sick as a rotten fish!

"I hope the crew wake up soon," Inna said. "The *Sea Rat* is starting to swirl."

"Aye!" I said, looking out to sea. Clegg was trying his best to steer the ship, but soon it was going to be too late. If the crew didn't come to help, we were going to sink!

Just then, I saw Aaron and Vicky racing toward us. But there was one problem . . . Rotten Tooth was racing right behind them!

"Get back here, ye little thieves!" he shouted. He looked meaner than a school of angry sharks! He grabbed Aaron with one hand and Vicky with the other. I thought he was going to toss them overboard right then and there.

"I think we're in trouble now," Gary said.

"Aye," I said. The rest of the crew had

woken up, too. They were starting to come above deck. And they didn't look too happy.

"Our treasure's been stolen!" they said.

"AYE! It be those pollywogs who stole it," Rotten Tooth roared. "Stealing from sick pirates—ye'll be walking the plank for this."

"Blimey, I think we're doomed," Gary whispered.

"Aye," I agreed, staring at the angry crew.

Suddenly, a voice boomed, "Unhand those li'l shipmates!" It was Captain Stinky Beard! He'd woken up, too. "We'll all be swimming for our lives if we don't man the sails!" he bellowed.

For the first time since coming on deck, the sleepy crew noticed the ship was spinning.

Rotten Tooth dropped Aaron and Vicky. "We'll deal with this later," he warned us before running off to help set the ship back on course.

Chapter 10
Smooth Sailing

The crew tugged this way and that way. Then they tugged that way and this way. It took forever, but finally the *Sea Rat* was out of the whirlpool's current.

"Looks like we saved the ship just in time," I said to my friends.

"Aye, just in time for Rotten Tooth to toss us overboard," Aaron said.

Rotten Tooth stumbled over to where we were standing. "Arrr! Mayhaps we should be leaving ye back there in Serpent's Whirlpool?" he growled.

"Mayhaps not!" Inna shouted at him.

"Aye," Vicky agreed.

"Aye, we saved the ship!" Aaron added.

"QUIET!" Rotten Tooth roared. "Ye

stole, and stealers walk the plank!" The whole crew was gathered around us.

"We weren't stealing," I tried to explain. "The treasure was cursed! That's why the whole crew got seasick."

"Aye!" Inna said. "We had to take the treasure so everyone would wake up. It was the only way to keep from sinking."

"Hogwash!" Rotten Tooth said. "There be no curse on that there treasure."

"Then what about the crabs?" Gary asked. "Pirate legend says that means the treasure is cursed."

"Aye, and Clegg says the same thing," I added.

Clegg was still at the wheel and the crew took us over to him. Then they asked Clegg if we were telling the truth about crabs and cursed treasure.

"Aye, it be a true fact that crabs only guard cursed treasure," Clegg told the crew.

"Those are just silly stories," Rotten Tooth said. Then he grabbed Aaron and me and hoisted us up in the air.

I gulped!

I thought we were going to be shark bait for sure!

"Unhand our wee mates!" Captain Stinky Beard ordered.

"But Cap'n, they stole," Rotten Tooth said.

"Aye," the cap'n agreed. "But if ye had reported to me about the crabs in the first place, I'd have known that treasure was never supposed to be found."

"Aye?" I asked.

"Aye," Captain Stinky Beard said. "Once again, ye shipmates have proven yourselves to be shipshape pirates."

We all smiled real proud.

Captain Stinky Beard ordered the crew to reverse course. "We're going to return to that island and rebury the treasure," he said. The crew were more than happy to obey. They'd had enough of being icky sicky.

"We're sorry, mateys," they told us. "We should've known ye would never steal from us."

"Aye," Captain Stinky Beard said. "As a reward, ye each may take one piece of treasure from the ship's treasure room."

"Hooray!" we shouted. Then we danced around a little bit. It was the most special reward a pirate could get. Every pirate on the *Sea Rat* gave us three cheers. Every pirate but Rotten Tooth, that is. It made him grumpy whenever we were right and he was wrong.

"I know what I'm going to pick," Inna said. "A shiny pin to wear on my best dress."

"I'm going to pick a golden spyglass," I said. I couldn't wait to climb up the crow's nest and peek through it.

Gary said he was going to pick a book of pirate legends. "They might come in handy one day."

"Aye," Vicky agreed. She said that she and Aaron were going to pick matching swords.

"Aye," Aaron said, pretending to swing around an invisible sword. "And then I'm going to use it when Rotten Head teaches us how to swashbuckle!"

We all giggled watching Aaron jump around.

That's when Rotten Tooth leaned over and growled in Aaron's ear. "Aye? Well, matey, ye'll *never* get to use it, then," he said. "Because ye pollywogs won't be  learning to swashbuckle for a very long time! Our deal is off! Today's school lesson is for ye lot to clean that stinky mess hall."

Inna, Gary, and I moaned and groaned as Rotten Tooth stumbled away. Aaron and Vicky were giggling, though.

I couldn't believe my ears.

"What's so funny, mates?" I asked.

Vicky uncovered her mouth and whispered to us, "We only took four sets of boot buckles before Rotten Tooth woke up," she said.

"Aye," Aaron said. "So Rotten Guts over there is going to be a little icky sicky until we tell him."

"Mayhaps we'll let him know once we get ashore." I giggled.

"Aye!" My friends giggled back.

It was a little mean, but it only seemed fair. After all, Rotten Tooth had sort of stolen the boot buckles from us, and stealing is against the pirate code. That was a Pirate School lesson that Rotten Tooth still needed to learn.